About the Author

Patricia Callendar was born in the UK and now lives on a small island off the west coast of Canada.

NIGHTINGALE PAPERBACK

© Copyright 2021
Patricia Callendar

The right of Patricia Callendar to be identified as author of this work has been asserted by her in accordance with the Copyright, Designs and Patents Act 1988.

All Rights Reserved

No reproduction, copy or transmission of this publication may be made without written permission.
No paragraph of this publication may be reproduced, copied or transmitted save with the written permission of the publisher, or in accordance with the provisions of the Copyright Act 1956 (as amended).

Any person who commits any unauthorised act in relation to this publication may be liable to criminal prosecution and civil claims for damages.

A CIP catalogue record for this title is
available from the British Library.
ISBN 9781838751074

*Nightingale Books is an imprint of
Pegasus Elliot MacKenzie Publishers Ltd.
www.pegasuspublishers.com*

First Published in 2021

**Nightingale Books
Sheraton House Castle Park
Cambridge England**

Printed & Bound in Great Britain

Patricia Callendar

Dragon Stories 1
Dogon

Nightingale Books

For Paul

There once was a small dog-like dragon named Dogon. He had a black velvety head with floppy ears and enormous, soulful brown eyes. And he had a short spiky tail which he could wag just like a dog. He was a sort of seeing-eye dragon and had been trained to help fire-breathing-impaired elderly dragons find their way through the dark forests. His fiery breath was brighter than bright and could send out shafts of firelight showing the passageways through the great tree branches. For many of the oldies this would be a treacherous journey because their fiery breath had sputtered to merely a smoldering glow and they would bump into the branches and tree trunks.

Dogon was also bilingual and could speak dragon English and dragon French. When at work he would roar cheerily, "Alors, mes amis, suivez-moi!" and the old dragons would fly confidently behind him. "Here you are guys," he'd say on arrival, "safe and sound. Have a nice day. A bientôt!"

They would roar back at him, "Thanks, Dogon."

"A votre service!" he'd reply, and then he'd fly off to find his pals for a game of dragon tag or just to hang out in the upper branches of the biggest trees and chat.

It was a good life, but Dogon was restless and always looking for adventure. He often had dreams of exciting events, but could rarely remember them afterwards.

One night, however, Dogon had a very vivid dream and it was still crystal clear in his mind when he awoke. He had dreamed that he was a real black Labrador puppy belonging to a small boy. In this dream he romped and chased balls; he gnawed on raw meaty bones; he swam in a lake, and he curled up at the end of the boy's bed every night. It was a lovely dream.

However, as he rubbed his eyes and blinked in the early morning shafts of sunlight, Dogon found himself still in the familiar Dragonland forest, breathing fiery smoke rings into the cool morning air. He felt bored and discontented. This particular day he wasn't needed for guide dragon duty and his friends were all busy. He flew aimlessly on auto pilot out of the forest and off into the far distance where he'd never been before, practicing doggie growls and woofs, swishing his spiky tail in circles, rolling over for imaginary tummy rubs, wishing he had a small boy to play with and a ball to chase.

Suddenly, because he wasn't concentrating, one of his wings brushed against the branch of a huge dragonapple tree and knocked a big rosy red apple flying. Dogon's eyes widened in excitement and he dived after the apple, accelerating downwards at great velocity. He caught the apple, spun around, lost his balance and plummeted down, down, down into a sparkling ocean. Sploosh! Aaarrghh! Splutter! Gasp!

He surfaced, flailing his great sodden wings in an effort to take off, but the water held him down. So he thrashed around with his legs, toes splayed out like fins and – miracle! – he was swimming… doggie paddle! He blew out fiercely in excitement, but nothing but damp steamy air escaped. Oh dear. His dragon fire power was extinguished. Continuing to swim, and still flapping his wings to dry them, he headed towards a sandy shore. He waded out of the water, cold and dripping. He shook himself all over. The spray went far and wide ….

"Hey! Don't do that!" came an indignant shriek. A small boy had been crouching down by some tide pools collecting special pebbles, sea glass and shells into a big red bucket, but now, glaring at Dogon, he stood up, the sea water spray dripping off his orange sun hat, and waved his arms in defiance. "I'm soaking! And who – oh, well, actually, *what* are you anyway?"

"So sorry," said Dogon. And then, as an afterthought, "uh, er, um, je suis désolé, monsieur. Parlez-vous français?"

"Non," said the small boy, "well, you know, un peu, but not much really. I'm Paul."

"Very pleased to meet you, Paul," said Dogon. "My name is Dogon and I'm a bilingual seeing-eye dog-dragon."

Paul stared up at Dogon in astonishment and admiration. His eyes were as big and round as saucers. "A real dragon? I love dragons. But why were you swimming? And can you breathe fire?"

Dogon looked dejected. He explained to Paul about his dream and the huge red apple and his big swim in the ocean and how the sea water seemed to have extinguished his fiery breath. Paul was sympathetic and suggested that they should sit on the beach in the sunshine so that they'd both dry out and maybe Dogon's breath would become fiery again.

They found a huge driftwood log further up the beach. Paul climbed up and sat on top of that while Dogon lay down in the sand. This way they could communicate fairly well without Paul getting too much of a crick in his neck. They chatted for a long time, sharing stories and experiences. Dogon's wings dried out and he felt warm all through … but no flames came out of his mouth.

He had told Paul all about his guide dragon job, realizing that he could no longer do that if he couldn't breathe fire. Paul screwed up his face in concentration and thought for a while. "What do dragons eat?" he asked eventually. "Because my dad grows wonderfully fiery hot chili peppers, and if you ate some of those maybe they'd reignite your breath!"

"I eat anything," said Dogon, "but I've never had chili peppers before."

"Stay right here," said Paul, "and I'll be back very soon. I wonder how many you'd need?"

"Rather a lot, I would think," said Dogon doubtfully, "maybe you shouldn't bother. You might get into trouble." But Paul was gone, up the beach and up some wooden steps to the seaside cottage where he lived with his parents and baby brother. In the vegetable garden he studied the bushy pepper plants. There were lots, and each one had quite a few glossy fruits – red, yellow, green, orange.

Paul didn't know which types were the hottest (he didn't like hot peppers, only the sweet bell types), but he knew some would be VERY hot – his dad was always discussing habaneros versus poblanos, jalapenos and others. Carefully he picked some of the reddest and ripest-looking peppers, stuffing them into the pockets of his shorts

When he had picked seven he thought he'd better not take any more so he headed back to Dogon on the beach.

"Try these," he said to his new friend. Dogon carefully took all seven chili peppers in his dog-dragon claws and popped them into his mouth.

"Yum!" he said. Paul waited. Dogon waited. Then he burped and breathed out slowly. A teeny red glow emerged with a teeny puff of smoke.

"Yay!" shouted Paul as he jumped up and down in excitement. "It worked!"

Dogon jumped up and down in excitement too (creating quite a crater in the sand), and with each upward bounce his breath became fierier and smokier.

"Thank you Paul, so very much. Merci, merci beaucoup!" Then he realized that the sun was way off in the western sky and that the day was passing quickly. "Oh dear, I must hurry home for guide dragon duty at sundown," he said. "Shall we meet again?"

"Oh yes," said Paul, "of course we must meet again, but I don't think I can promise any more hot chili peppers, so please don't let your fire burn out! My dad may be a little suspicious when he sees some missing in the garden, but I expect I can explain. I'll tell him some weird and wonderful story about a dragon and he'll scratch his head, raise his eyebrows and laugh. I love my dad." Then, rather shyly, he added, "Au revoir! That means see you again."

The friends parted with big smiles and waves. Paul collected up his red bucket and headed home. Dogon flew up and over the ocean back to the Dragonland forest, breathing out fiery flames and barking like a black Labrador puppy. Both were happy with memories of a special encounter and hopes of more to come.